SULLiVAN'S iSLAND LiGHTHOUSE

H.L. HUNLEY SUBMARiNE

N

W   E

S

'SLAND LiGHTHOUSE

ATLANTiC OCEAN

Happy Reading!

THE ADVENTURE BEGINS

HERMY THE HERMIT CRAB

BY ANDREA WEATHERS / ILLUSTRATION BY BOB THAMES

Andrea Weathers

LEGACY PUBLICATIONS

5-09-05

WHEN HERMY THE HERMIT CRAB was a baby hermit crab, he lived in the warm water of the Atlantic Ocean – just off the coast of Charleston, South Carolina. He was very tiny at this first stage of his life, measuring only 1/8 of an inch in length. He was called a zoea. (Pronounced zo-EE-a.)

Hermy spent these carefree days eating and floating along with his brothers and sisters, hidden in a clump of Sargassum Seaweed that provided food and shelter for the growing crabs. They were drifting towards Folly Beach.

As Hermy ate and grew larger, he molted to shed his outer covering, known as his exoskeleton. (Pronounced EX-o-SKEL-e-ton.) Then a new one grew in its place.

BUT HERMY WASN'T HAPPY. You see, the young hermit crab did not weigh enough to sink to the bottom of the ocean. Hermy wished that he were older and bigger so that he could travel on four of his own legs. It was hard for Hermy to be patient and not to be in such a hurry to grow up. And he didn't have a place to call home.

As Hermy passed by the narrow island of Folly, the rhythmic sounds of beach music drifted across the water from the Folly Beach Fishing Pier. Smiling couples were dancing the Shag, while a pair of Dancing Dolphins jumped above the water. And Hermy grew a little larger.

IN CHARLESTON HARBOR, Hermy approached the point of the peninsula known as the Battery. Several Sassy Seagulls stood on the sturdy railing, just waiting to spot a fish below. And Hermy grew a little larger.

TWO HANDSOME HORSES pulled a covered carriage down East Bay Street past the
historic three-story homes with their joggling boards and hidden flower gardens.
And Hermy grew a little larger.

THE OLD EXCHANGE BUILDING still housed a dimly lit dungeon in its damp basement. Hermy shuddered when he thought of the fearless pirates, like Stede Bonnet, confined here at one time for their crimes. A colorful Majestic Macaw perched on his stand. And Hermy grew a little larger.

OUTSIDE A SMALL GROUP OF PEOPLE gathered on the sidewalk.

A Curious Cat, sitting beside a lamppost, listened to a favorite Charleston ghost story.

And Hermy grew a little larger.

AT THE OLD MARKETPLACE on Market Street, Hermy watched the talented ladies weaving and selling their handmade Sweetgrass baskets. A hungry flock of Plump Pigeons hurried about the street for scraps of food. And Hermy grew a little larger.

AT THE CHARLESTON MARITIME CENTER, a family of Awesome Otters played alongside a visiting tall schooner. And Hermy grew a little larger.

HERMY ADMIRED THE GREAT BLUE HERON in his outdoor home on the top floor of the South Carolina Aquarium. And Hermy grew a little larger.

ACROSS THE COOPER RIVER at Patriots Point, Hermy coasted past the Aircraft Carrier *Yorktown*. A Loggerhead Sea Turtle watched Hermy and his friends as they drifted by the stately ships. And Hermy grew a little larger.

HEADING SOUTH, HERMY GAZED UP at the Sullivan's Island Lighthouse.

A local fisherman and his Respectful Retriever motored past Hermy in their fishing boat.

And Hermy grew a little larger.

FINALLY, HERMY ENTERED HIS last stage of childhood and became too heavy to stay afloat anymore. Now he was known as a Megalops. (Pronounced MEG-a-lops.)

While Hermy was several miles south of Sullivan's Island, he sank to the bottom of the ocean. Well, almost to the bottom. Hermy landed on a rusted iron shipwreck, half buried in the mud, that obviously had been here for many years. Why, Hermy was sitting on top of the famous Confederate submarine named the *H.L. Hunley*! Now what would he do?

HERMY SLID DOWN the curved side of the famous sub to the ocean floor. The happy hermit crab tried out his two pairs of walking legs for the very first time. They worked! Now he was free to walk wherever he wanted to go without having to depend on the ocean currents for transportation.

Hermy felt great respect for this place, where the *Hunley* had rested since February 17, 1864. He made a mental note to remember where this sub was located.

BUT HERMY HAD A NEW PROBLEM, now that he was a juvenile crab. The back of his body was soft, and he needed protection from his predators. Hermy had to scurry across the sandy floor of the ocean and hide, rather quickly, under a bright yellow bush coral to escape the watchful eyes of a Suspicious-looking Spadefish. He needed something to wear on his back, something that he could also carry with him.

WHILE EXPLORING NEAR FOLLY BEACH, Hermy wandered about the rocks and corals and couldn't believe his eyes. He discovered a whole community of hermit crabs, just like him, but sporting many different kinds of shells. They came in all sizes and shapes. There were Snail shells, Periwinkle shells, Whelk shells, Tulip shells, and many others. Hermy knew that he needed one of these colorful shells. And he wanted to fit in and become a part of this group.

A FELLOW HERMIT CRAB, in an Atlantic Moon Snail Shell, had just discovered an empty Whelk shell. He was measuring the vacant shell with his two antennae and front pincers. Then he jumped out of his shell and into the empty one so fast that Hermy almost missed the exchange. The hermit crab must have liked the new shell, because he darted away, leaving the old one behind.

HERMY APPROACHED THE ABANDONED SHELL and looked it over. It seemed to be about the right size. It was a very pretty beige shell marked with violet swirls, resembling a shark's eye. He liked the outside and decided to climb inside for a peek. The inside was smooth, and it fit just fine. Hermy held on to the shell with his smaller, back legs. He stuck his longer, front legs out and took a few steps. To his surprise, walking with the shell on his back was easy. Now Hermy had a house for protection—one that he could carry with him.

HERMY WAS EXHAUSTED from the excitement of seeing the sights of Charleston, learning to walk, discovering the lost *Hunley* submarine, and finding his first shell and a place to call home. Growing up was a wonderful adventure. He backed all the way inside his new house, blocked the entrance with his larger claw, and settled down for a much-needed rest.

Goodnight, Hermy!

ANTENNAE / The hermit crab has two antennae, which are used to measure the inside of a prospective new shell, and they act as sensory devices that detect substances in the water.

ATLANTIC MOON SNAIL SHELL / A smooth, single spiral shell, tan in color, marked with colored bands of blue-gray to brown, very common on South Carolina beaches. The darker center swirl and round shape give the appearance of an eyeball—hence, the nickname "Shark Eye." Its size can be 1/4 of an inch to 5 inches in diameter.

ATLANTIC OCEAN / The large body of salt water touching the Eastern shore of the United States.

BEACH MUSIC / A type of rhythm and blues music with a relaxed 4/4 time that originated in the 1940s. It could only be heard from jukeboxes, mainly at the beach piers and pavilions of the Carolinas, and was therefore called "beach music." Its popularity increased in later years with hit songs from bands such as the Embers and the Tams.

CARRIAGE TOUR / One of the most relaxing ways to tour downtown Charleston is in a horse-drawn covered carriage. The licensed guide knows about the city's architecture, history, sites, and trivia.

CHARLESTON BATTERY / This area of the Charleston peninsula, where the Ashley and Cooper rivers meet to form the Atlantic Ocean, is commonly referred to as White Point Garden or Battery Point. The seawall on the East Bay Street side is referred to as the High Battery, and the Murray Boulevard side is called the Low Battery. The term "Battery" reminds us of the past presence of the military stronghold that protected Charleston.

CHARLESTON HARBOR / The body of water that lies inland from the Atlantic Ocean, formed by the Ashley and Cooper rivers bordering the peninsula of Charleston. All large ships enter the seaport through the channel in this harbor.

CHARLESTON MARITIME CENTER / Located near the South Carolina Aquarium, the center features docking for visiting tall ships, tugboats, barrier island tour boats, etc. It will be home to the schooner *Spirit of South Carolina*, currently under construction.

CHARLESTON, SOUTH CAROLINA / One of the oldest cities in the United States, settled in 1670. Charleston is a seaport situated on a small peninsula of land laced with marshes and beautiful beaches. This charming city offers locals and tourists many historical sites and magnificent architecture in churches, homes, gardens, plantations, forts, monuments, and shops.

CONFEDERATE / Pertaining to the union of Southern states, 1861–64.

CORAL / A colony of tiny sea animals that grows in the shape of a bush with many branches. The coral that washes up on Charleston area beaches is called Sea Whip Coral, in colors of yellow, orange, red-burgundy, and white.

DOLPHIN / The bottle-nosed dolphin is the most common aquatic mammal in S.C. waters. It appears to be smiling.

EXOSKELETON / The supportive outer covering of a hermit crab or other animal.

FOLLY BEACH, SOUTH CAROLINA / The city, located on the barrier island of Folly, is only 20 minutes south of Charleston and is a favorite family vacation destination.

GHOST STORY / Colonel Isaac Hayne was an American patriot whose ghost is believed to haunt a room on the third floor of the Old Exchange Building. Colonel Hayne was kept there to await his hanging in 1781. Folks say that they have seen his ghost pacing back and forth at the window.

GHOST WALK / A walking tour led by a licensed guide through the historic district of downtown Charleston. Tales of haunting and the presence of ghosts are told at the sites where they are said to have been seen.

GREAT BLUE HERON / A large, shy bird with long legs, neck, and bill that feeds in shallow water but nests in trees.

HERMIT CRAB / A common crab in the shallow waters of the Carolinas. A hermit crab's natural shell is shed through a process called molting when the shell is outgrown. The back of its body is soft and needs protection from its predators; therefore it must seek a shell discarded by another animal such as a snail. When the crab outgrows its adopted shell, it must find a larger one.

HISTORICAL / Something that has its base in the past. Many Charleston homes and buildings are considered historical because they were built in the 1700s and 1800s and are worth preserving for future generations.

H.L. HUNLEY SUBMARINE / The Confederate sub that successfully attacked and sank the USS *Housatonic* on February 17, 1864, just four miles south of Sullivan's Island. She signaled to shore after the attack, but never made it home. The *Hunley* was named after Captain Horace L. Hunley from Alabama, who died on the sub during one of its test runs. The wreck of the *Hunley* was raised in August 2000, and now rests in a special tank in the Warren Lasch Conservation Center while the conservation process continues. For more about the submarine and how to see it on weekends, see www.hunley.org.

JOGGLING BOARD/A much-loved Charleston tradition since the early 1800s. The joggling board is part bench and part rocker, up to 16 feet long, and common on Charleston piazzas. One bounces gently on the sturdy, solid pine board, which is painted Charleston green, of course! It is said that if a couple start out on opposite ends of the joggling board, they will meet in the middle.

JUVENILE CRAB/A crab that is not yet fully grown into adulthood.

LOGGERHEAD SEA TURTLE/The most commonly seen sea turtle in the waters off the South Carolina coast. This cold-blooded, air-breathing reptile with a backbone lives in the open ocean. The females return to the beach from May to September to lay eggs.

LOWCOUNTRY/The low-lying land in South Carolina near the marshy coast of the Atlantic Ocean.

MACAW/The scarlet macaw is a member of the parrot family and is a native of the area from eastern Mexico to Brazil. This large bird nests in tall trees and features a massive beak, long tail feathers, and bright blue, yellow, red, and green feathers.

MARKETPLACE/The Charleston City Market is a major shopping area for unique Charleston items, such as jewelry, nautical crafts, T-shirts, artwork, and sweets. In its early form, it was a produce and seafood market for Charleston's first families.

MEGALOPS/The second stage in a young hermit crab's life.

MOLT/The process by which a hermit crab sheds its outer covering.

MOON SNAIL/A mollusk with a smooth, single spiral shell.

OCEAN CURRENT/The strong flow of ocean water in a definite direction.

OLD EXCHANGE AND PROVOST DUNGEON
Completed in 1771 as the Customs House and Exchange for Charles Towne. The basement exposes part of the original walled city of Charles Towne and the Half Moon Battery. The water in the basement reminds us that the land behind the building is a result of filling in over the years.

OTTER / A furry mammal with webbed feet for swimming and a slightly flattened tail.

PATRIOTS POINT/ Home of the popular Naval and Maritime Museum on the Cooper River in Mount Pleasant.

PENINSULA / A body of land that is almost completely surrounded by water. The Charleston peninsula is a good example.

PERIWINKLE SHELL / A small, gray spiral shell that once housed a living Marsh Periwinkle Snail.

PIGEON / A common bird in Charleston parks that will feed aggressively on bread, French fries, chips, etc.

PINCER / The front pair of a hermit crab's legs has pincers that are used for feeding, defense, and to block the entrance to its shell.

PIRATE/ A sailor who plundered ships and towns for wealth. When caught, a pirate was locked in the Old Exchange Building to await trial and possible hanging from the oak trees in Whitepoint Garden.

PREDATOR / An animal that feeds on another. A hermit crab's predators are shorebirds and fish.

RETRIEVER/ The golden retriever is a large breed of hunting dog with a thick, golden coat. It is used to retrieve waterfowl.

SARGASSUM / A floating, brown seaweed originating in the Sargasso Sea of the Gulf Stream. It has a long stem with flat leaves and branches of small air sacs that resemble berries.

SCHOONER / A sailing ship with two or more masts.

SEAGULL / The herring gull is the most common species found in South Carolina. It is a large gray bird with a white head and chest, pink legs, and a yellow beak that features a red spot on the lower part. These gulls do not dive completely into the water for food, but scavenge for food on shore.

SHAG / The official state dance of South Carolina.

SHARK EYE / Another name for the Atlantic Moon Snail Shell. The center of the spiral is dark brown and black, resembling an eye of a shark.

SOUTH CAROLINA AQUARIUM / Features aquatic habitats native to South Carolina's mountains, Piedmont region, coastal plain, coast, and ocean.

SPADEFISH / A disc-shaped fish with sharp-spined fins, found along the waters of the south Atlantic coast. It resembles the angelfish with its bold stripes of silver and black.

STEDE BONNET / Known as the "gentleman pirate" because he came from a good family and did not need to turn to piracy. He served in the British Army, and acquired wealth legally before becoming a pirate. He was hanged in Charleston in 1729.

SULLIVAN'S ISLAND / A barrier island off the coast of Mount Pleasant.

SULLIVAN'S ISLAND LIGHTHOUSE (OR CHARLESTON LIGHT) / Built in 1962 to replace the Morris Island Lighthouse. It is 163 feet tall and its cross section is triangular. It is the only lighthouse in the United States with an elevator. Its light can be seen 26 miles out to sea. Since 1963, when the Morris Island Light was turned off, this light has blinked twice every 30 seconds to warn approaching ships of land.

SWEETGRASS / A type of long blade grass that grows in the Low country and is used for weaving baskets. Pink to lavender blooms are visible in the fall. The Lowcountry is the only place in the world where this African form of art and craft is still practiced and handed down from one generation to the next.

TULIP SHELL / There are two kinds in the Carolinas. The common Banded Tulip has seven distinct brown lines around it and reaches 4 1/2 inches in length. The less common True Tulip has 15 circling lines and reaches 9 to 10 inches in length.

WHELK / A very large marine snail with a spiral shell. The Knobbed Whelk is the most common whelk shell on Charleston's coast, with knobs along its spiral lines and its opening on the right. The inside opening is orange and white. The outside displays vertical lines of purple to brown.

YORKTOWN AIRCRAFT CARRIER / Known as the "Fighting Lady" of World War II, commissioned April 15, 1943, it is the flagship of the Patriots Point fleet.

ZOEA / The first stage of a hermit crab's life.

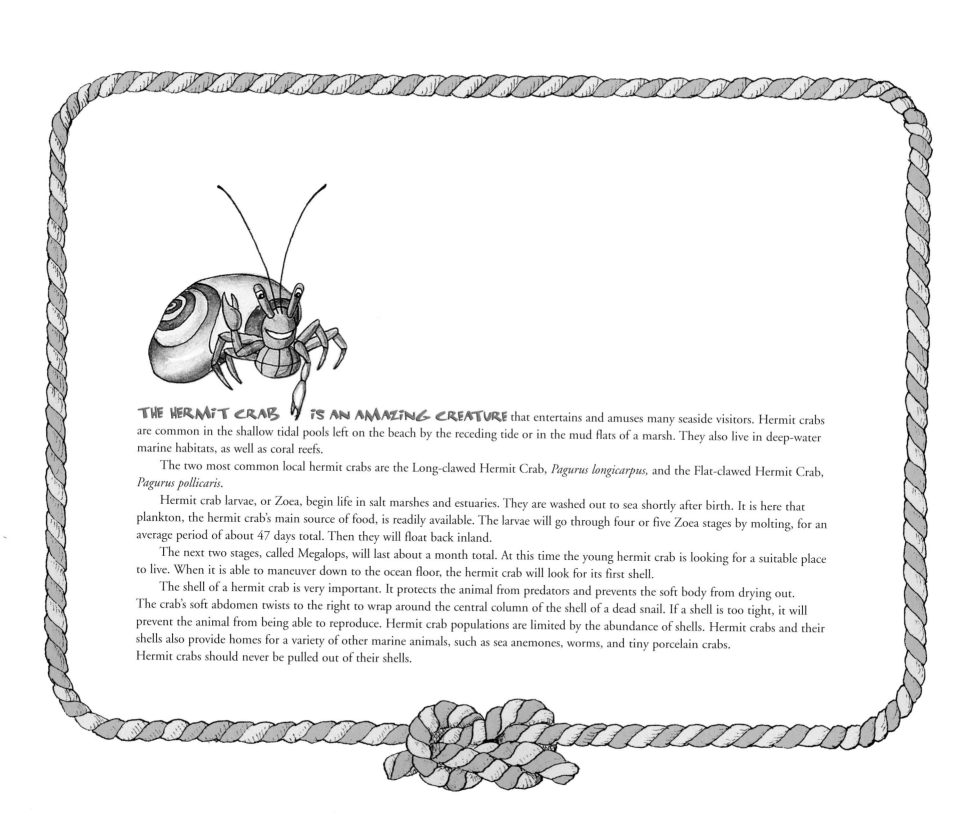

THE HERMIT CRAB IS AN AMAZING CREATURE that entertains and amuses many seaside visitors. Hermit crabs are common in the shallow tidal pools left on the beach by the receding tide or in the mud flats of a marsh. They also live in deep-water marine habitats, as well as coral reefs.

The two most common local hermit crabs are the Long-clawed Hermit Crab, *Pagurus longicarpus,* and the Flat-clawed Hermit Crab, *Pagurus pollicaris.*

Hermit crab larvae, or Zoea, begin life in salt marshes and estuaries. They are washed out to sea shortly after birth. It is here that plankton, the hermit crab's main source of food, is readily available. The larvae will go through four or five Zoea stages by molting, for an average period of about 47 days total. Then they will float back inland.

The next two stages, called Megalops, will last about a month total. At this time the young hermit crab is looking for a suitable place to live. When it is able to maneuver down to the ocean floor, the hermit crab will look for its first shell.

The shell of a hermit crab is very important. It protects the animal from predators and prevents the soft body from drying out. The crab's soft abdomen twists to the right to wrap around the central column of the shell of a dead snail. If a shell is too tight, it will prevent the animal from being able to reproduce. Hermit crab populations are limited by the abundance of shells. Hermit crabs and their shells also provide homes for a variety of other marine animals, such as sea anemones, worms, and tiny porcelain crabs. Hermit crabs should never be pulled out of their shells.

I dedicate this book to my mother, Muriel Anne Edge Weathers (1931–74), whose love for the beach brought me to Folly Island,
to my father, Darus D. Weathers, who helped my mother to realize her dream of living on the beach,
and to my stepmother, Cathy Weathers, for keeping us all together. – AGW

I dedicate this book to my loving wife and daughter, Karen and Amy. – RET

Special Thanks to . . . LARRY DeLANCEY, Crustacean Monitoring Supervisor at the South Carolina Department of Natural Resources,
for sharing his in-depth knowledge of invertebrates and reviewing the text and illustrations. ALLEN STELLO, historical tour guide at the
Old Exchange and Provost Dungeon, for his ghostly knowledge of Isaac Hayne. BRIAN BARRACLOUGH, STEVE JANTZEN, and CARL PARRISH for
the use of their boats for the Sullivans Island Lighthouse illustration. HARRY PECORELLI, Staff Underwater Archaeologist at the Warren Lasch
Conservation Center, for his amazing diving story at the Hunley site. ERIC COUCH, CCPRC Assistant Manager of The Folly Beach Fishing Pier,
for his loyal devotion to keeping Hermy in stock and his quick wit and comments. SAM at Patriot's Point Gift Shop, PATTI at Barnes & Noble,
RICH at Historic Charleston Foundation, SARA at Preservation Society of Charleston, Luden's Marine Gear, CLAUDIA at Aquarium,
MARGE at Waldenbooks, and all who carry the books and plush Hermy. GLORIA ASKINS, Director of Admissions, First Baptist Church School,
for her support, her love for AW's children, and her charming personality. BOB HUDSON, our publisher at Legacy Publications,
for his constant support and wonderful sense of humor. DAVID BROWN, Legacy's production director, for handling all of the logistics.
JAIMEY EASLER, our art director at Legacy, for his great work and innovative ideas. SARAH LINDSAY, our copy editor at Legacy,
for her research abilities. DARRELL W., A.W.'s brother, for being "Hermy's uncle." LINDSEY and MILLIE for all of their thoughts and support.

Legacy Publications, 1301 Carolina Street, Greensboro, NC 27401 / www.pacecommunications.com
Printed in Canada by Friesens

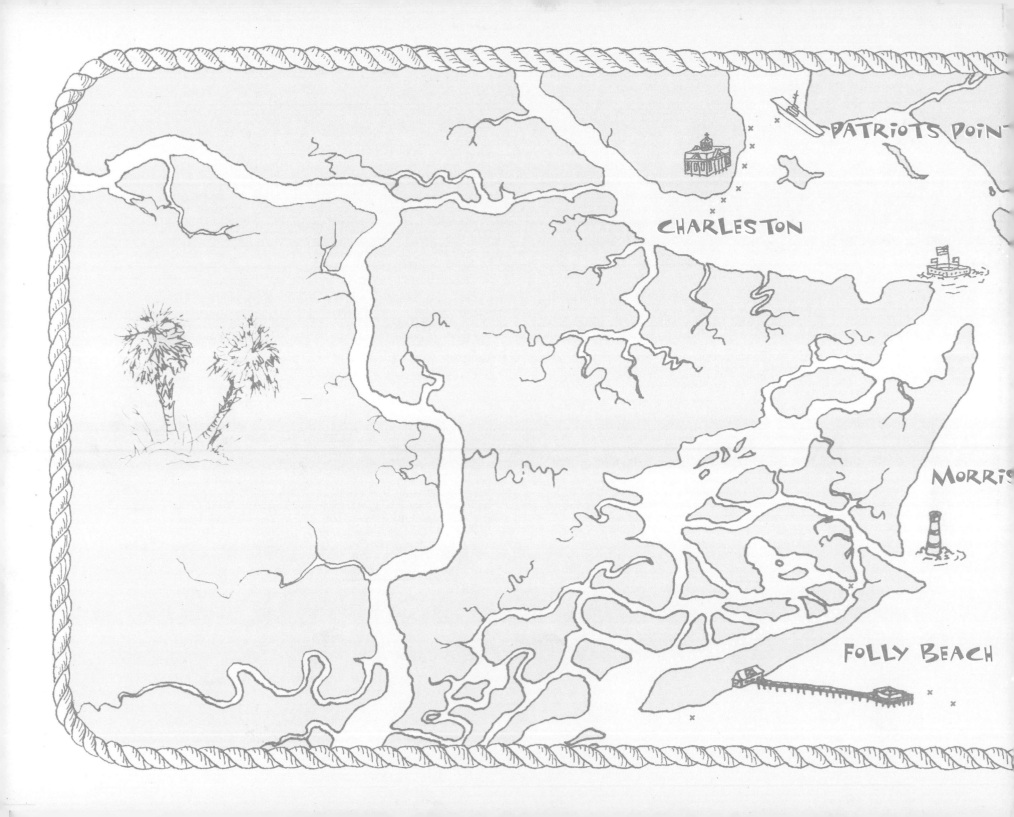